Tips for Reading Together

Children learn best when reading is fun.

- Talk about the title and the pictures on the cover.
- Look through the pictures together so your child can see what the story is about.
- Read the story to your child, placing your finger under the words as you read.
- Have fun finding the hidden caterpillars.
- Read the story again and encourage your child to join in.
- Give lots of praise as your child reads with you.

Children enjoy reading stories again and again. This helps to build their confidence.

Have fun!

Find the caterpillar hidden in every picture.

Dad's Birthday

Written by Cynthia Rider
Illustrated by Alex Brychta

OXFORD
UNIVERSITY PRESS

It was Dad's birthday.

Dad had a cake.

He had a bike.

He got on the bike.

"Go on, Dad," said Biff.

"Go on, Dad," said Chip.

"Go on, Dad," said Kipper.

Dad fell off!

Oh no!

Think about the story

How did Dad make the children laugh when he was on the bike?

Why did Dad fall off the bike? Why isn't it a good idea to stand on a bike like that?

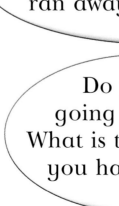

How do you think everyone felt when Floppy ran away with the cake?

Do you like going to parties? What is the best party you have been to?

Matching

Match the parcels to the presents.

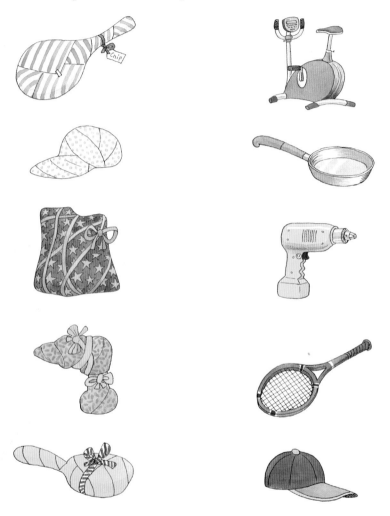

More books for you to enjoy

Level 1:
Getting Ready

Level 2:
Starting to Read

Level 3:
Becoming a Reader

Level 4:
Building Confidence

Level 5:
Reading with Confidence

OXFORD
UNIVERSITY PRESS

Great Clarendon Street,
Oxford OX2 6DP

Text © Cynthia Rider 2005
Illustrations © Alex Brychta 2005
Designed by Andy Wilson

First published 2005
All rights reserved

British Library Cataloguing
in Publication Data available

ISBN 978-0-19-838556-1

10 9 8 7 6 5 4

Printed in China by Imago

Have more fun with Read at Home